ISBN: 978-1-7354493-0-2
Library of Congress Control Number: 2020921959

BELLA AND THE TREASURE TREE

This book is dedicated to Victoria, Autumn, Olivia, Hunter, Alyssa, and Haven; who let me journey this life with them through their eyes.

Let your imagination take you on your own journey.

Author
Melissa Sprabary

Bella couldn't believe this day was here. She was leaving her childhood home, the big exciting city, and all her friends behind. She was never really bored for any period of time. She always had something to do, somewhere to be, and someone to do things with. Now, her family would be moving to the unknown, and she knew it would never be the same.

Bella's mama, in all her excitement, noticed Bella's tears. She knew that this would be a big change for her little girl. Her mama asked if she could have just a little hope. It may not be as bad as Bella thought it would be. Bella said she would try.

Bella was happy her mom was going back to her own childhood home, but would Bella be able to fit in and meet new friends? Would they like her or think she was different from them? Bella told her mama she would give it a chance, but just as soon as Bella thought things would work out, they pulled onto a long country gravel road.

She thought to herself that maybe they were taking a short cut. There was nothing surrounding the gravel road on either side but a bunch of overgrown trees. She softly asked her daddy if they were lost. Daddy smiled and said they were almost there, just a few more miles. Those few miles seemed like days. Bella couldn't believe there wasn't a house, a barn, a shed, or a dog house anywhere in sight. The land was completely covered in trees.

Finally, after a long journey down the country road, they pulled up onto a large, old looking home. It almost looked like a life size doll house. Bella asked her mama if this is where she grew up, and with a smile, Mama replied, "Thankfully, yes." Bella didn't know what to think of it all. This was completely opposite of where they used to live.

As they unlocked and opened the door, they stepped inside to see that it was just as if someone still lived there. Every room was painted or decorated differently. One was decorated and painted with animal's from a wild safari. Another room was painted with a swimming pool with giant floats made of sea creatures. The largest room was painted like an amusement park with large ferris wheels, roller coasters, balloons, and carriages full of cotton candy. It was all so beautiful and not like any home she had ever seen.

Bella then climbed the wooden staircase that creaked all the way up to the entrance of her new room. It was the biggest bedroom she had ever seen. Its walls were bright pinks, yellows, and purples and painted with lovely flowers. It had shelves full of musical carousels, and beautiful vases sitting throughout the room to hold fresh cut flowers. There were doll carriages scattered around the room and a lovely tea table in the corner. It was the best room ever!

Her mama came up and said, "This was my room as a little girl, but you can make it all your own. We can paint it different colors and add your dolls if you want," Mama suggested. "Oh no, Mama," Bella stated. "This is exactly how I want my room to look." Mama smiled as she looked at her precious angel, remembering the time when she was her daughter's age and the life that she had found in this place.

As the small family started to unpack and organize, Bella asked her mom a question she had been wondering while she was unpacking her room. "Did you have any friends here, Mama?" she asked. "Oh yes!" Mama replied. "I had so many friends that I could barely keep up with them all!" she continued. "Wow," Bella said in an almost unbelieving voice.

"So, where did you find them?" Bella asked curiously. She knew they could not be anywhere close by. There was nothing but trees for miles. "Well, at school and at other places," Mama said confidently. "You will have a chance too. Just remember what I always say.

Keep your heart and mind open to what God wants to show you, and who He wants to bring into your life," said Mama. Bella smiled. It seemed to be enough to satisfy her for the moment as they continued decorating their new home.

After several days of making the house their own, Bella asked Mama how it was that the house she grew up in seemed to be just as she had left it. Mama responded, "Well, Nana and Papa left it for me because they always knew how much I loved the house and I wanted to come back someday," her mama said. Bella could not imagine why they would want to come back. It was an amazing house, but that's all there was. They were miles from town, and they had no neighbors at all close by. The only animals she found around the house were the usual squirrels, birds, and an occasional raccoon that liked their leftovers in the outside trash can.

Bella's mama could sense her daughter's questions and knew that this was a big change from what Bella was used to. Her daddy and her mama tried to keep her entertained with movie nights in their living room with popcorn and candy, playing board games, and playing hide and seek. However, her mama could tell that Bella was getting bored really fast. Bella was very good at entertaining herself, but there were only so many imaginary stories she could tell her dolls before a kid just goes stir crazy being cooped up too long. Bella's mama couldn't wait for her little girl to find the same happiness in this place that she had as a young girl.

The following morning, her mama asked Bella if she had taken a walk out in the yard. "What for?" Bella questioned. "There's nothing out there but trees!" she explained. "Well, perhaps if you were to look harder you could find something to entertain you. Use your imagination," Mama suggested. Bella wasn't too thrilled at the idea of roaming around in and out of a bunch of old trees but decided she needed some air anyway, so out she went. "Remember to stay inside the fenced yard, Bella!" Mama shouted as Bella set outside. "Yes, ma'am," Bella responded. As Mama watched her daughter walk out the back door, Mama smiled a big smile. She had a feeling something special was about to take place.

Bella had the whole day ahead of her as she started walking with her head facing the ground. After a while, she didn't know how far she had gone, so she looked up to make sure she was still within the fence. "I'm still good," she said to herself. As she continued pacing and wandering around, she thought she heard something that sounded like music. She couldn't quite make it out, but it sounded like something from a music box.

Maybe there was someone out there she could meet. The music was faint, but she tried really hard to listen and walk closer to the sound. She kept walking and walking, and the music became louder and louder. But, she still could not tell where it was coming from. As she stopped to listen more closely, she closed her eyes. With her hands out as if playing hide and seek, she walked forward towards the sound dodging and ducking in out of the trees until she finally made it.

Once Bella opened her eyes, she couldn't believe what she saw. In an instant, there was a huge clearing of open sky and right in the center of this clearing was the biggest tree she had ever seen in her life. The tree trunk was the size of her school playground back home, and the branches were almost as large as the trunk in size. The giant branches swooped all the way down to the ground and went as far up as the eye could see. It was the most magnificent tree she had ever seen.

After staring in amazement at such a glorious tree, she remembered the music and could hear it quite plainly now. Surely this tree doesn't play music, she thought to herself. Perhaps there is someone up in the tree with a music box. "HELLO!" she shouted. "ANYONE THERE?" she shouted louder but no reply.

As she hollered for a while with no response, she guessed there must be a tree house built up high within the branches. Maybe the owner could not hear her because of the music. So, up she went. Branch after branch after branch she climbed. The music became louder and louder, and she knew she was getting close. Bella came to a stop and found what looked like a large, hollow room within the tree. As she gazed inside the room, there was a maze of spiral stairs carved within the tree. The spiral of stairs went way down deep down into the tree, and all the way up as far as the eye could see.

As Bella began to climb the stairs, she saw what looked like a candle beaming within. As she got closer and closer to the light, she stopped suddenly and gazed in amazement. Bella found the most incredible discovery. It looked like the inside of a pocket watch or like the inside of a music box, only multiplied one hundred times. It spread all throughout the inside of the trunk. There were hundreds and maybe thousands of winding wheels, springs, levers, hinges, bells, and whistles. Some were gigantic in size and some as small as a thimble. Each was made of beautiful gold, brass, and silver. They all ticked and tocked, clinked and clanked, and chimed together making their own music in full harmony.

As Bella sat in awe watching the beautiful masterpiece, she looked around for anything that could be responsible for this: maybe a magician, or an artist, or an architect. Only to find no one. She could not find an explanation. This just had to be a dream. The longer she sat, the more her eyes grew sleepy. The sight and sounds were so enchanting that it started to put her into a sound sleep.

Just then, a dong from a bell woke her wide awake. Bella saw an opening just below her coming from inside the tree itself. It was just like an opening from a cuckoo clock. It would close and open just as a bird would perch about its base. "That's impossible!" she said out loud, and it was then that she heard what sounded like laughing from inside. Then, someone spoke, "Anything is possible my dear!" came a voice chiming from the ledge of the base. Bella thought she would faint if not for her curiosity getting the better of her.

"Who's there?" Bella questioned. "Well, my name is La Rue, but everyone calls me Rue," came the reply. "Are you just going to sit there, or are you going to come in?" Rue asked. Bella thought for a moment and was a little frightened. Rue could sense the hesitation and decided to properly introduce herself. Rue didn't come out much because there really was no reason to come outside of this tree, but she made the effort for Bella.

All at once, a kangaroo popped out from inside a room onto a ledge where a bird would normally be. She had a baby in her pouch. "Hello, little one!" shouted Rue. "Welcome to our Treasure Tree," she continued. "I've introduced myself, and this little guy here is my baby, Pocket's. I named him Pockets, well, because he stays inside my front pocket." Bella just couldn't believe what she was hearing. Rue was talking like a person. Bella felt no threat at all from Rue, so she decided to introduce herself. "My name is Bella," she replied. "Well, it's very nice to meet you Bella," said Rue. Little baby Pockets stretched out his little finger to shake Bella's hand.

"If you would like to come inside, you can meet all the others," Rue said to Bella. "There are others?" Bella looked in shock. "Why of course," Rue laughed a little. "I understand being afraid of the unknown, but I should reassure you that there is always a way back outside anytime you wish to leave," Rue assured Bella.

"You see the branches here?" asked Rue. Each one of them has what you call knots, but they actually are exits to leave the tree. You can go out as you please, but you must enter only from inside the clock here. That's for our protection, you see," Rue explained. Bella thought for a moment and then decided to go inside. "I can only stay a little while," said Bella. "Stay as long or as little as you like," said Rue with a smile.

As Rue directed Bella inside the opening of the tree, Bella could hear the sounds of laughter and music of a different tune. It was most beautiful and like nothing that she had ever heard. She could smell fragrances of baking, candies, campfires, and flowers. She could see colors dancing all around her: some popping bright from side to side and up and down while some quiet and faint and still. She could hear musical instruments coming from all throughout the tree. Melodies unlike anything ever heard. It was a wonderful sensation to have all her senses going at the same time.

It was an amazing feeling. She felt quite safe and warm and even most welcome here, surprisingly so. "Okay there, Bella," said Rue, "Let me give you the short guided tour. Here we have all these branches in our tree. Each branch has a special place, event, or time. You can choose to visit all of them or pick a favorite and stay as long as you wish. The choice is yours," Rue continued.

"Each one has a special door to enter, you see, not one is the same," explained Rue. "But, there are so many branches," Bella stated. "How can I choose, and I would not have the time to see them all," Bella suddenly felt very sad. "Oh, no worries child," assured Rue. "If you have the time in your life, you can visit as often as you like," said Rue.

Bella hadn't thought of coming back time after time. But, after all, this tree was in her own backyard. How she never saw it before was beyond her, but she was suddenly grateful. "That would be wonderful, thank you," Bella smiled. "Now, which of the branches would you like to visit first?" asked Rue. "It's so hard to choose," added Bella. "Perhaps you could show me which door has that amazing fragrance?" asked Bella. "But, of course," assured Rue. "Excellent first choice," she added while baby Pockets was nodding in agreement.

As Rue, Pockets, and Bella went up and down and all around, they came to the door Bella chose first. Rue looked at Bella and suggested she take all the time she wanted. Then, Rue explained that if she needed her at any time, just say her name, and she would come hopping right to her. Bella smiled and thanked her.

As the door to the branch slowly opened, Bella was overwhelmed with glorious scents. She slowly walked in and moved forward to a golden light shining bright. With each step, it became brighter and brighter. As she came to the entrance, it all suddenly appeared before her.

It was, to her surprise, a beautiful open field that went for miles and miles straight into the sky. It was filled with the most beautiful wild flowers she had ever seen. The colors were rich, bright, and alive. They all looked so happy. The dancing display of all the different flowers swaying together made her want to sway right along with them.

There were Virginia bluebells, tiger lilies, night caps, blue bonnets, daisies, fairy slippers, orchids, cherry blossoms, moon flowers, pink ladies, and kitten tails. Every scent you could imagine floated above their blooms.

As she stood in silence embracing the glory of it all, a large, turquoise and black butterfly the size of her hand, and a cluster of lovely red and yellow ladybugs came to introduce themselves. "Hello, Bella. My name is Mose," said the kind butterfly. "And, we are the Ladies of the Flowers," said the ladybugs all at the same time. "We are so pleased you could come! We are here to escort you through our home if we may?" they asked Bella. "Oh, I would love that, thank you," she replied.

As Mose and the Ladies of the Flowers gathered on each side of Bella, they took the sleeves of her dress and lifted her gracefully off the ground. She felt like an angel with wings soaring above the beauty of the flower fields beneath her. Mose and the Ladies of the Flowers gently placed Bella on a cloud of feathers hovering about as if waiting for her arrival. It was so soft and squishy and felt just like her pillow at home.

As Mose and the Ladies of the Flowers joined Bella upon the cloud of feathers, she could feel a moist breeze and hear the sound of a babbling brook from a stream ahead. As they sailed softly closer, there were magnificent willow trees on both sides of the brook. These trees were nothing like she had ever seen. Their branches were filled with a dazzling display of bird houses, not one of them the same. Some had baskets of birds' nests filled with babies chirping and calling their mothers for food and attention with their beaks open wide.

The willows were also filled with fluttering and busy nightingales, swallows, blue jays, red robins, orioles, cardinals, and hummingbirds. These creatures were of brilliant colors: Crimson reds, Castleton greens, royal purples, violet blues, and sun fire yellows. They all fluttered about whizzing by Bella to welcome her and say their hellos.

The water from the brook was so clear that she could follow their reflections dancing in the rays and beams from the sun. She could see turtles and fish touching the surface ever so closely to see if a bird would drop a worm or two for their delight. The lily pads were filled with frogs floating and hopping, in hopes of catching a passing fly.

Mose and the Ladies of the Flowers carefully lowered Bella to the bank of the brook. She took off her little sandals and placed her toes in the coolness of the water. It was delightful and refreshing as the pebbles swayed ever so gently beneath her feet. Mose and the Ladies of the Flowers sat gently upon her shoulders. They were making funny and silly faces to see their reflections in the water causing Bella to laugh with delight.

Bella felt like she was inside a dream. This was by far the most glorious place she had ever seen or could ever imagine. The sweetness of this place took her breath away, and even for someone so small and young such as herself, she felt this life of wonder and beauty inside her little heart.

This suddenly became a part of her life that she wanted to hold snuggly and safely inside her forever. She never wanted to forget this moment. As the time seemed to stand still so that she could capture all its wonder and imagination, she knew she needed to get back home. Even though she could stay there and rest in the scents, the sounds, and the joy of this place, she believed what Rue said: that if she ever wanted to come back again, she was always welcome.

She called for Rue who suddenly appeared popping and hopping from feather cloud to feather cloud. With baby Pockets snug as a bug inside his pouch laughing, smiling, and taking in the sights and sounds in his own way, they made their way to Bella. "Rue," Bella said softly, "This is one of the most amazing and unbelievable days of my life." "It was a lovely place to start," replied Rue. "But, there is so much more for you to experience," she continued.

"I know the day is coming to an end, and you must be getting back home. We hope to see you again someday soon," Rue stated, with baby Pockets nodding in agreement. "Oh, I certainly hope so too," Bella smiled back. Bella said thank you and goodbyes to all her new found friends: Mose, the Ladies of the Flowers, and all the birds of the trees. She still could not believe all that had happened, but indeed it had, and she wasn't about to forget any of it as long as she lived.

After locating the exit from the branch, Rue carefully opened the hatch and out Bella went waving happily back to Rue and baby Pockets who waved back. Down and down the branches she went, each seeming more alive to her than before. What a most impressive, special tree I found, she thought to herself. While on her way back home, she was thinking back to the beauty, the scents, and the new friends she made that day. She would never forget it. She could hardly wait to go back again and see what else the tree had waiting for her.

She thought of telling her mama all about her adventure, because she told her mama everything, but was sure her mama would think it a great story of her imagination. She decided she would keep it her big secret and treasure it in her heart for now. Maybe someday, she could share it with others, but this was her adventure that she wanted to explore herself.

When Bella got home, Mama asked Bella how her day had gone. Bella responded that it was very surprising. When Mama asked her if she wanted to tell her about it, Bella simply said, "Maybe someday." Mama didn't press, and it really took Bella by surprise that her mama didn't question her more. But, in a way, she was relieved that Mama didn't press her further.

Bella woke the next morning and she felt so alive inside. She was dressed and down for breakfast in a matter of minutes, and Mama asked Bella what she had planned for the day. "Oh, just to take another walk in the yard," she responded. Mama told her that she would be right here if she needed anything and to have fun. She was glad Bella wanted to be outside more. Bella said she would be home by supper and gave Mama a big hug before she left.

When Bella arrived at the tree and looked upon the size and awesomeness of it, she wondered for only a moment if it was all real. But it didn't take her long this time to reach the massive chiming pocket watch. She waited patiently for the bell to dong and the opening of the tree to appear. She could still hear the sweet melody of the music coming from within, just as it was yesterday.

As the bell rang out, the tree immediately opened up. Once inside, she met Rue and baby Pockets waiting for her. "Good morning, child," stated Rue. "It's so nice to see you this fine morning," she continued. "It's a lovely day to explore something new or perhaps go back and revisit the same place from yesterday?" she asked Bella.

"I think I would like to find something new today, Rue," Bella answered. "Magnificent!" Rue exclaimed. "Go ahead and pick a door, any door, and we'll be right here when you're ready," Rue assured her as before. "Thank you, Rue. I will see you all in just a while," Bella replied and took off like a flash of lightning. She could hardly wait and could only imagine what each branch would show her.

Bella ended up at the lower branches today instead of staying at the middle like yesterday. As she approached the towering door, it slowly began to open.

She lightly stepped inside, as if she did not want to wake anyone. She again came to the opening. She found a fruit filled vineyard to her left and a towering rainbow of an orchard to her right. It was filled with every fruit that existed, and the smell of the ripe, juicy fruit was so inviting. The vineyard was covered in berries that popped in a kaleidoscope of colors.

As she stood there trying to take it all in, an upside-down umbrella floated down to her. She looked in shock, and once it landed in front of her, she saw six of the tiniest little finches. With them were plum and apple seeds, fig and persimmon seeds, and every seed that comes from fruit. "Hello, Bella. I've been expecting you," said one of the finches. "My name is Pipit. All my sisters and I gather all the seeds and pits from the fruit when they are ripe and ready to be picked, and then we replant them. If you want to jump in, we can take a trip through the vineyard and orchards if you like," Pipit offered.

Bella thought for a moment how these tiny birds could carry an umbrella upside down with all these seeds plus herself. She thought she could almost see Pipit smiling a little bit at her, as if she knew what she was thinking. She finally agreed, and she climbed inside. Amazingly, the finches had no problem carrying her, the seeds, and the umbrella which was a great relief to Bella.

As they glided easily along, they went into the vineyard first. She was amazed at the sight. Miles and miles of vines full of plump and bright blueberries, dewberries, raspberries, gooseberries, huckleberries, boysenberries, juicy watermelons, and strawberries. Each one was almost jumping and swinging from their vines waiting to be picked and enjoyed.

The vines were covered in bumble bees and honey bees, each one taking their turn, almost smiling while picking ripe berries and placing them inside tiny buttercups. They would then carry them off to be prepared for treats and delights. It was an unusual but most exciting sight to see.

Next, they glided over the towering orchard trees. Their branches beheld bubbles of rainbow colors: apricots, Clementine's, cherries, sweet figs, sugar apples, peaches, oranges, pomegranates, jujubes and sweeties. This was a sight to behold!

Storks were flying above and below the branches allowing the ripest and juiciest of fruits to be dropped inside their large beaks and then carried away for feasting. It was so alive and touching to see how carefully the fruit and vines were so loved by those taking care of them. Each one was filled with excitement to be savored and enjoyed to the fullest.

Bella knew this was a special place. This was the fullness of God's creations: the fruits of the earth, each one different from another, just like Bella who is like no one else. Pipit asked Bella if she would like to see the assembly, and Bella was eager and very excited.

Pipit and her friends carried Bella to what looked like an old general store. It was the kind of store that had old toys, candies, and games that you couldn't find anywhere else. When she climbed out of the umbrella and walked in, the sweet scents of pies, pastries, and cakes were making her mouth water with delight.

It was a store as big as her house and every corner and every shelf was overflowing with peach cobblers, blueberry and boysenberry pies, and coconut and raspberry cakes. Another side was filled with blackberry and grape jams and jellies, and berry butters served over warm, fresh homemade breads.

Another side was filled with fresh, ready to serve fruits and berries to prepare any kind of smoothie or ice cream shake one could imagine. One room was a giant candy land. Not just any candy, but only candy made of fruits and berries: persimmon pockets, laughy taffy, huckleberry hoops, plum sickles, pomegranate pops, apricot cotton candy, and maple pear syrup over coconut canes.

Bella never thought of fruit and berries to be so special. She delighted herself with many of the treats and treasures inside the store. Pipit and her sisters joined Bella in singing and whistling a beautiful melody all their own. It was quite magical how they all sang and whistled the same songs. They blew bubbles the size of balloons and floated about the delightful creations picking candies here and there all throughout the store.

Bella was having the most wonderful time but needed to get back home to call it day. Pipit and her sisters floated Bella back to the knot exit, gave her little pecks of kisses on her nose, and wished her a good night. They hoped to see her soon again, and Bella assured them she would return. Bella started her way back home, and in the sunlight, she found herself wishing she had someone to share this adventure with.

She thought of her mama and played the conversation out loud. The more she tried to describe her new treasure, the more joy filled her heart. She thought she would wait a little longer before she decided to tell anyone.

Little Bella went back to the Treasure Tree as often as she could and experienced life in the fullest. She went to oceans, to jungles, to the mountains, and on a safari that turned into a giant, alive, amusement park. All the animals she could ride just like a rollercoaster, or a swing, or fly high above in the sky. She had not realized it yet, but it was just like some of the rooms that were painted inside her own home.

Her favorite place was when she found Heaven. It was a paradise like no other. It had the biggest playground she had ever seen with children playing all around, and she made more friends than she could ever count. The angels had wings that could cover her entire house, and they would carry her wherever in Heaven she wanted to go. She met Jesus, and He told her how much He loved her and all the little children. Bella enjoyed everything she experienced within the treasures of her tree.

On Bella's sixteenth birthday, her mom had something very special planned. She had invited all their family to come to the house to celebrate with Bella. Bella was so tempted to take everyone she loved to the tree, but she still hesitated. Bella often wondered why her mama had never mentioned the tree to her. Bella thought it was certainly a tree worth talking about and surely her mama had found it herself, but she never said anything about it. Perhaps one day she would ask her mama, but maybe another day.

As the family began to enjoy the party and fellowship together, Bella slipped off to visit Willow. The Treasure Tree family always had very special surprises for her on her birthdays, and she couldn't wait to see them.

As Bella started towards the opening where the tree was, her mom and Nana walked up behind her. Bella thought she would faint, but her mom said everything was okay. She asked Bella, while smiling, what she thought of the tree. Bella looked wide-eyed at her mom and Nana grinning sweet, questioning smiles.

"You know about the tree, Mama?" Bella asked, almost crying, she was so happy. "Yes, sweetheart," her mama stated. "Both Nana and I played in this tree when we were little girls: first Nana, then myself. This is why it was so important for me to come back and raise my family here.

When I finally got the nerve to bring Nana here, she had told me that she once wrote a book of all her adventures in the tree. I thought it was the most wonderful idea and started writing my own as well. We would love it if you wanted to read our journeys' and share your own someday," Mama stated. "I would love that too, Mama," Bella expressed with love and laughter.

"Where do you think the tree came from, Mama?" Bella asked. Bella saw her mom look at her Nana with a sweet smile. Nana told Bella that the tree was where God the Father, Jesus, and His Spirit express their own life inside us. The roots of the tree are like God the Father. They have the perfect foundation for beautiful ground and soil to dig deep, stay strong, powerful, and healthy. With God as the root in our life, no storm will ever blow us away or separate us from God.

The trunk is where Jesus and His Spirit breathes and gives life to us so that we can dance, sing, praise, and worship. We as His children are the tree's branches. As long as we stay with Jesus, His Spirit, and God the Father, we will always have His life inside us. He will show us how to live and how to love. He will teach us how to use all our gifts to be creative, to be adventurous, and to share His love with the whole world.

This is His beautiful gift to us. Isn't it the most beautiful gift?" Nana asked with the most loving smile. Bella hugged their necks, and they all cried together while La Rue, baby Pockets, and the whole Treasure Tree family watched quietly, simply beaming with joy and happiness for the best birthday gift Bella could ever receive. The adventures of the Treasure Tree would live on.

The End

This book takes you and your child on a journey through life as far as you want your dreams and imagination to take you. Experience life through the dreams of your child as they explore the life that's expressed within their hearts. Let them dream through this book of what it would be like to go where they want to go and do what they want to do, and share this with you.

Bella and The Treasure Tree is my heart and joy; writing through the eyes of my step daughters, nieces and nephews. They have taken me along with them throughout their lives and I could not ask for a greater gift.

I would like to share my stories with the greatest gift we've been given on this earth; children. Through their innocence and pure eyes, I want their imaginations to come to life. I hope you enjoy these stories as much as I am blessed to receive them from my Lord and Savior, Jesus Christ.